Big Yang
and
Little Yin

Written by Angela McAllister • Illustrated by Eleanor Taylor

For Tazzi and Harriet,
with thanks
A.M.

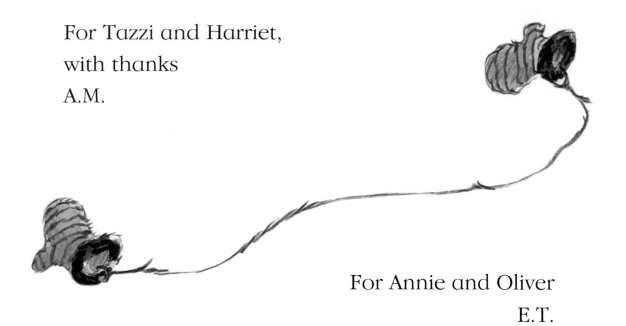

For Annie and Oliver
E.T.

Big Yang
and
Little Yin

Written by Angela McAllister • Illustrated by Eleanor Taylor

Big Yang and Little Yin were playing brave explorers.

"Let's explore the forest," said Little Yin.
"Yes, that's the place for adventures!" said Big Yang.
So Little Yin put her blankie into her wagon, and off they went.

Soon they found a
perfect tree to climb.
Big Yang pulled Little Yin up
onto the lowest branch.
"I want to climb higher,"
said brave Little Yin.

And with Big Yang's help she did.

Then they found a stream.

"Let's make a raft," said Big Yang.

So they turned the wagon upside down.

Big brave Yang paddled the raft around the rocks.

After a while they stopped to pick some berries.
All around, the forest creaked and rustled.
"What's that?" whispered Little Yin.
"Don't worry," said Big Yang.
"There aren't any fierce animals
in this forest."

"Brave explorers aren't afraid of fierce animals,"
said Little Yin.

6

Deeper into the woods they went.
Big Yang made them a den.
Dark shadows shifted between the trees.
"Who's there?" whispered Little Yin.
"Don't worry," said Big Yang.
"There aren't any witches in these woods."

"Brave explorers aren't afraid of witches,"
said Little Yin.

Further on, they came to an enormous hollow tree.
Little Yin climbed up and peered into the trunk.

"I think it's a monster's house,"

she said in her explorer's voice.
But suddenly she wobbled and

dropped her blankie inside.

"Don't worry," said Big Yang. "I'll get it for you!"

8

Big Yang climbed into the
hollow tree and found the blankie.
But he couldn't climb out.

"H

elp!"

cried Big Yang.

Little Yin peeped
through a hole.
"Don't worry," she said.
"I'll get some help."

Little Yin looked around
the deep, dark forest.
"Are you afraid?" asked Big Yang.
"Um . . . brave explorers are never afraid,"
said Little Yin, with a shiver.

Big Yang grabbed his mittens
and threw them out of the tree.
"Take these, Little Yin," he said.
"They'll keep you warm."

Little Yin set off
through the forest.
She came to
Big Yang's den.
Spooky shadows
danced all around.

Suddenly Little Yin
didn't feel brave any more.
She tried to sing a loud,
witch-frightening song,
but her voice was
very small.

In the hollow tree
Big Yang sat alone,
peeping through the hole.

"Maybe this *is*
a monster's house,"
he said to himself,
"and maybe he comes
home for lunch…"

Suddenly Big Yang
didn't feel so brave.
He tried to hum a loud,
monster-scaring hum,
but his voice was
very wobbly.

Little Yin stumbled on until she found the berry bush.
The wind howled through the forest like a fierce animal.
"I don't want to be an explorer any more," said Little Yin.
"I'm only brave with Big Yang to take care of me."

But Big Yang was huddled in the hollow tree.
What if Little Yin forgets where to find me! he thought.
Big Yang didn't want to be an explorer any more.
"I'm only brave with Little Yin to take care of," he said.

Little Yin sat trembling
in a pile of leaves.

Then she remembered
Big Yang's mittens.

She put them on.
The mittens were warm
and cozy. Little Yin smiled.
She felt as though Big Yang
were holding her hand.

Up she got.
"I can do it,"
she said bravely.
"I have to find help.
Don't worry, Big Yang."
And on she went.

Inside the tree, a teardrop
rolled down Big Yang's cheek.

He picked up the blankie
to wipe his eye.

It was soft and cuddly and
it smelled of Little Yin.
Big Yang smiled.
He felt as if Little Yin was
beside him.

"I'm not really worried,"
said Big Yang bravely.
"Little Yin will
be here soon."
And he practiced his
alphabet to cheer himself up.

Before long Little Yin came to the stream and there was her wagon, still upside down. She had forgotten all about it. "This is just what we need!" cried Little Yin happily.

When Big Yang heard the
rattling wheels he jumped up.
"Little Yin!" he cried.
"The wagon! How smart!"
"Will it help?" asked Little Yin.
"It's perfect!" said Big Yang.

Big Yang threw the end
of the blankie to Little Yin
and she tied it on to the wagon.

Together they
pushed and pulled
the wagon inside.

Then Big Yang stood on
the wagon, and climbed
out of the hollow tree.

He pulled the wagon
out after him.

"Thank you, Little Yin," said Big Yang, giving her a hug.
"Do you think you know the way home?"
"Oh yes," said Little Yin.
She put the blankie and the mittens
in the wagon and slipped her hand into his.

"Should we stop for berries on the way?" said Big Yang.
"Yes," said Little Yin.
"Exploring makes you very hungry!"

And with a yawn and a rumble of empty tummies
the two brave friends shuffled home.

24

Big Yang and Little Yin
Text Copyright | Angela McAllister
Illustration Copyright |Eleanor Taylor
The rights of Angela McAllister and Eleanor Taylor to be named as
the author and illustrator of this work have been asserted by them in
accordance with the Copyright, Designs and Patents Act, 1988

Published in 2016 by Hutton Grove
An imprint of Bravo Ltd.
Sales and Enquiries:
Kuperard Publishers & Distributors
59 Hutton Grove, London, N12 8DS
United Kingdom
Tel: +44 (0)208 446 2440
Fax: +44 (0)208 446 2441
sales@kuperard.co.uk
www.kuperard.co.uk

Published by arrangement with Albury Books
Albury Court, Albury, Oxfordshire, OX9 2LP

ISBN 978-1-910925-07-2 (hardback)
ISBN 978-1-910925-06-5 (paperback)

A CIP catalogue record for this
book is available from the British Library
10 9 8 7 6 5 4 3
Printed in China